PUFFIN BOOKS

Published by the Penguin Group:
London, New York, Australia, Canada,
India, Ireland, New Zealand and South Africa
Penguin Books Ltd, Registered Offices:
80 Strand, London WC2R 0RL, England

penguin.com

Manufactured in China
ISBN: 978-0-141-50021-8

First published 2006
Published in this edition 2007

1 3 5 7 9 10 8 6 4 2

Text and illustrations copyright ©
Michael Broad, 2006

To my friends
and family

MICHAEL BROAD

Broken Bird

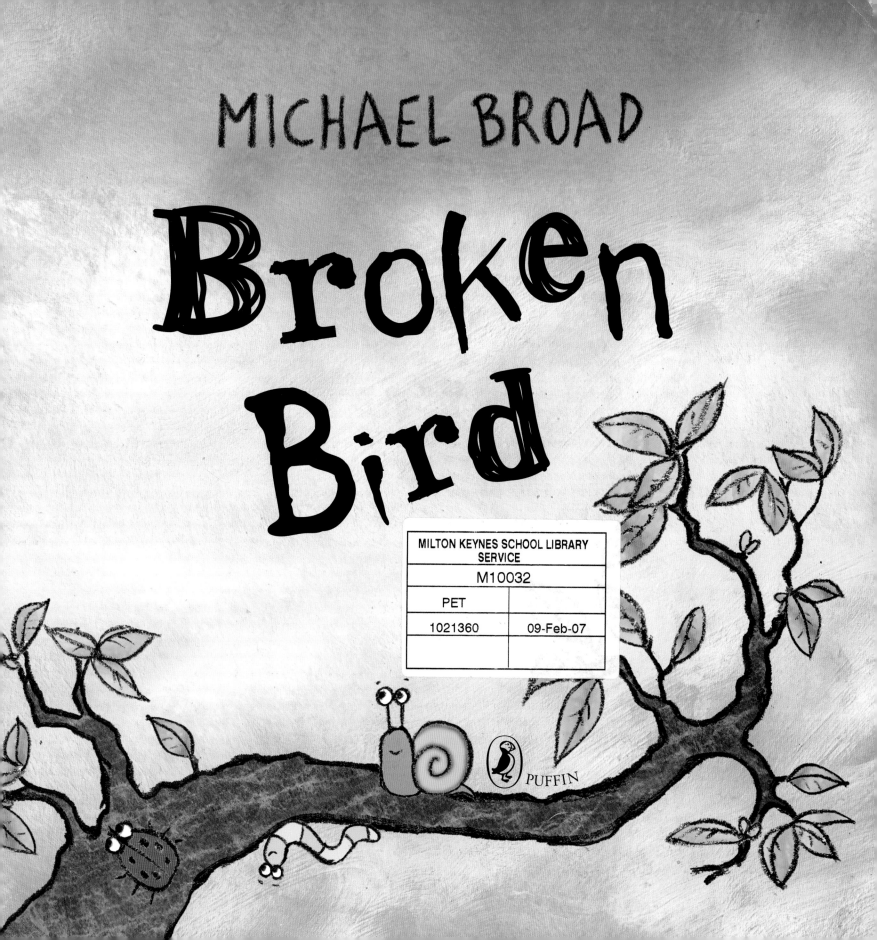

PUFFIN

When
Broken Bird
hatched from his egg,

he **didn't** know

he was **different**

from other birds.

It was only when his brothers
began to **point** and **laugh** at him
that he realized he **only** had
one wing.

Broken Bird

looked inside his shell to make sure
he had not left it behind,
but the other wing
was nowhere
to be found.

As time went by,
his brothers grew
big and **strong**,
gobbling up all the
fat juicy worms.

They didn't give
Broken Bird
a chance.

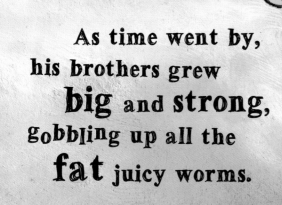

"You don't
need the best worms,"
they teased.

"You'll **never**
fly with just
one wing."

Poor
Broken Bird
was only left the
small **thin**
ones.

While both his
brothers learned to fly,

Broken Bird began to
build himself another wing.

But it wouldn't flap
and kept falling off.

A single tear rolled down
Broken Bird's beak.

The day came
when his brothers
started stretching
their wings to fly away.
Broken Bird was left all alone.

"Never mind," he said,
"I shall use my
two feet instead."

True, walking wasn't
as much fun as flying, but
Broken Bird
met lots of creatures along
the way who had no wings
at all.

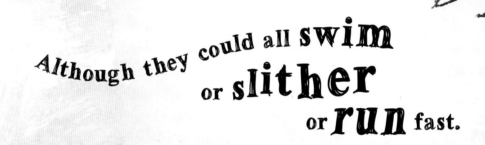

Although they could all **swim**
or **slither**
or **run** fast.

"I just don't belong here,"
sighed Broken Bird.
"Maybe . . ." he thought,
suddenly feeling better,
"maybe I'm a city bird!"

And he set off,
leaving the woods behind.

When he reached the city, it was night-time.

Broken Bird's legs were very tired.

It was very noisy and everything moved so quickly.

Broken Bird started to feel scared.

Broken Bird

looked for a quiet place to sleep,
away from all the bustle.

He whistled a happy tune
to cheer himself up.

Soon he realized
someone else was whistling too.

When he looked round, he saw a
yellow beak poking out
of a cardboard box.

"Hello," said Broken Bird.

"Hello," said the yellow beak.

"Why don't you
come out so that
I can see you?" asked
Broken Bird.

"Because I don't want to **scare** you," said the beak, from inside the box.

"You won't scare me, I promise," said Broken Bird, crossing the feathers on his wing.

The yellow beak belonged
to a yellow bird.
Broken Bird
thought she was
the most *beautiful*
thing he had ever seen.

"My name's
Broken Bird.
What's yours?"

"Scary Bird,"
she replied shyly.
"My sisters told me a bird with
one Wing would scare people away."

"I only have one wing too,"
said Broken Bird.
"My brothers told me
a bird that can't fly
must be broken."

They looked at each
other for a moment,
not knowing
what to say,
and then they
started **laughing**.

It was the first time **either** of them had **ever** laughed and they were not sure how to stop.

They talked and laughed until the sun came up.

In the morning,
Broken Bird
and **Scary Bird**
left the city and
returned to the woods.

Broken Bird showed his friend his favourite tree,

and they set to work

building a special nest.

Life was good.

And, after **lots** of practice,
and two very strong wings
between them . . .

. . . they even learned to fly.